The Lemonade Shop

Rosie Hankin

Illustrated by

Lynda Stevens

Our school is raising money for the children's hospital.
Today we are helping, too.

We're going to make
a shop and sell lemonade
to our friends.

How do we make lemonade?
We need to look in a cookery book.

Look for 'lemonade' in the index at the back of the book.

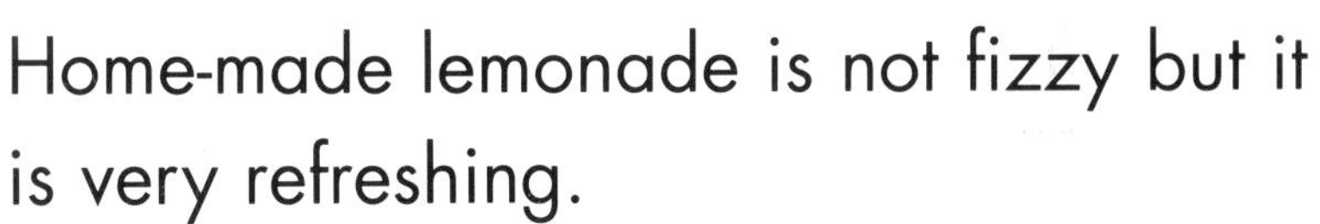
Home-made lemonade is not fizzy but it is very refreshing.

The recipe shows the ingredients for 10 cups of lemonade.

How much will we need for 30 cups?

I know, three times the amount.

Cookery books tell us what ingredients are needed and how to make the recipe.

We will need to buy 18 lemons.

What about the sug

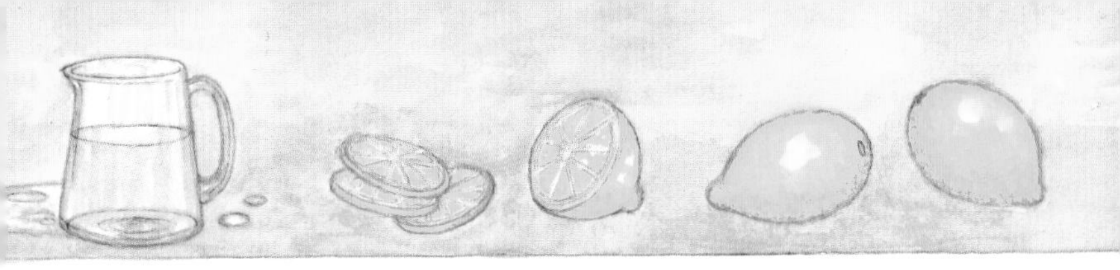

We'll need
450g of sugar.

Many recipes use sugar to make food and drinks taste sweet.

We're raising money
for the children's hospital.

Lemons are citrus fruits that grow in hot countries.

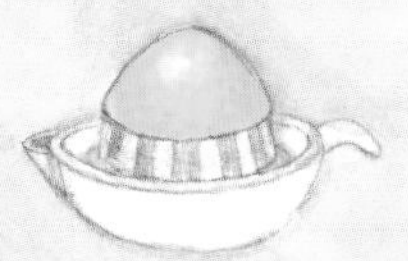

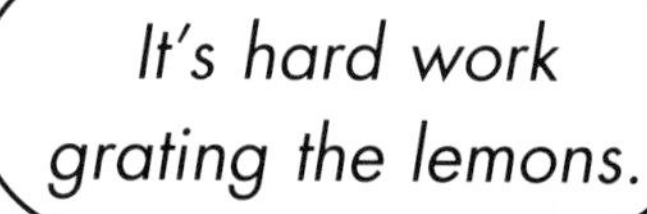
It's hard work
grating the lemons.

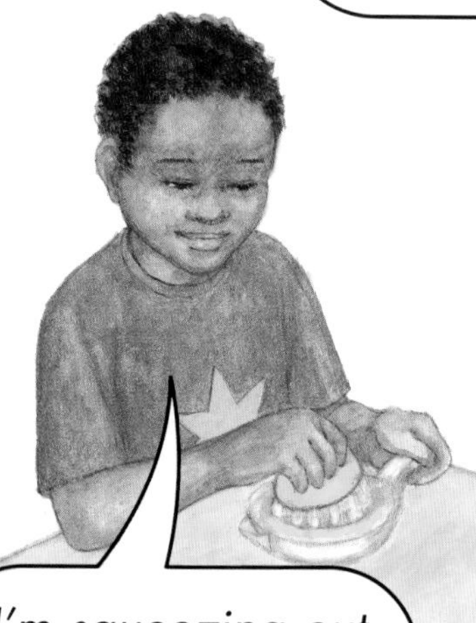

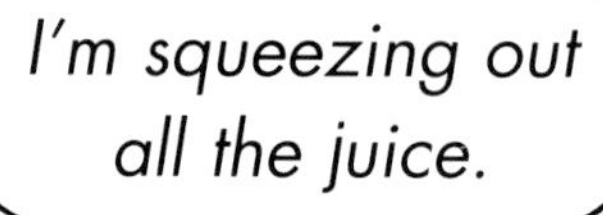
I'm squeezing out
all the juice.

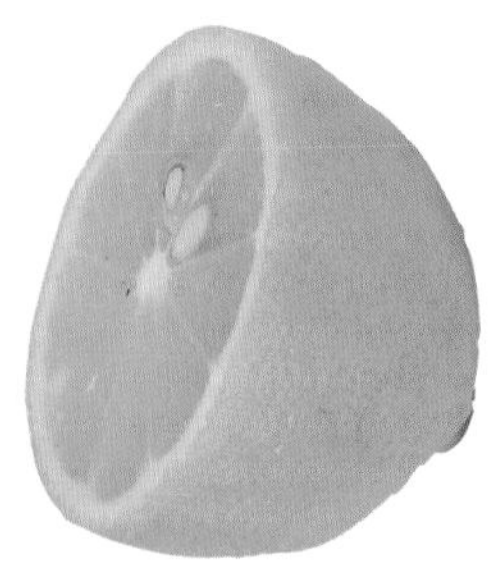

Mum is helping me to heat the sugar and water.

The sugar has to dissolve slowly in the water. The pan must not get too hot or the sugar might burn.

Put the lemon juice and rind in the sugary water.
Mmm, it looks really good!

To make any recipe you must use all of the ingredients and follow the instructions very carefully.

Now we can use some of the lemonade to make ice lollies.
Pour the lemonade into the lolly moulds very carefully.

The lemonade needs to cool in the fridge and the lolly moulds must go into the freezer.

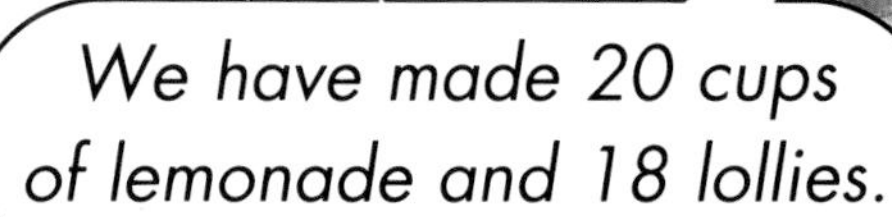

How much should we charge?

You should charge 25p for the lemonade and 10p each for the lollies.

We need to make a shop to sell our lemonade.
We can use the old kitchen table.

Put this sign on
the gate. It advertises
your lemonade shop.

This coloured paper will make our shop look nice and bright.
I'm writing out the price list.

We could use my toy till to put the money in.

I've got 40p. Please may I have a cup of lemonade and a lolly?

These lemon lollies are delicious.

That means you get 5p change.

We've sold all
of the lemonade
and lollies.

Well done! You've made £6.80.
We can take it into school for the children's hospital.

RECIPE FOR HOME-MADE LEMONADE

Ingredients for 10 glasses of lemonade

1.5 litres of water
150g granulated sugar
6 large lemons

Method

1 Grate the rind of the lemons and squeeze out the juice with the lemon squeezer.

2 Heat the sugar and water on a low heat until the sugar is dissolved. Be careful not to burn the sugary water.

3 Add the lemon juice and rind to the sugary water.

4 Carefully pour the lemonade into a heat-proof jug and place into the fridge. Strain the lemonade and serve chilled.

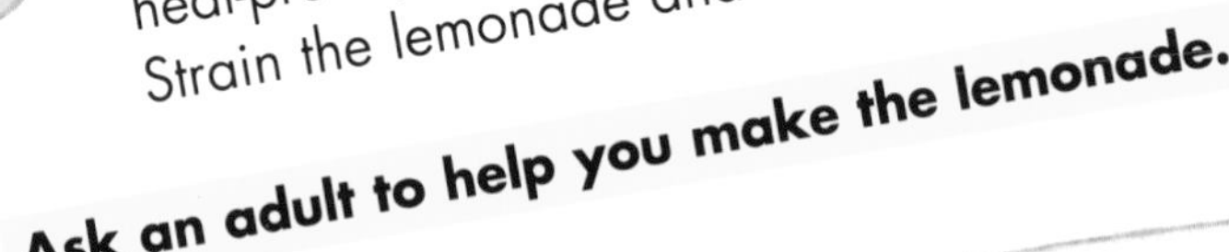

Ask an adult to help you make the lemonade.